PRAISE FOR BENJAMIN CARD

"Benjamin Card's stories are wide-ranging and very high-concept. He's a writer of true imagination."

—Kendare Blake, author of *Anna Dressed in Blood*

"While there's much here that will please Twilight Zone diehards, Card delves into a wide range of material with a voice that is wholly his own... Delightfully strange and psychotic."

—Hellnotes.com

"Card's bite-sized stories are inventive, compelling and prone to unforeseen twists and turns. Nothing is ever as it seems—the true mark of a talented storyteller."

—Jana Oliver, author of The Demon Trappers series

"Reminded me of why I loved horror novels in the first place... I couldn't tear my eyes away."

—OnlineBookClub.org

"Card's talent is self-evident, taking simple ideas and turning them inside-out, forcing the reader to re-evaluate what they thought they knew without being presumptuous or condescending. I'm excited to see what he comes up with next!"

—Jason Kristopher, author of The Dying of the Light series

"Card's voice is smart and accessible as he builds you up before dropping gut punch after gut punch."

—Stephen Williams, author of *Among the Ruins*

Villipede
PUBLICATIONS

Love
American Style

Benjamin Card

Published by **Villipede Publications**

Villipede Publications
PO Box 3643
Idaho Falls, ID 83403
villipede.com

Special discounts are available on quantity purchases. For details, contact the publisher at the address above or by email.

Printed in the United States of America

ISBN-13: 978-0692595749
ISBN-10: 0692595740

For My Family,
because when I fall
it's on you

INTRODUCTION

I would normally shun the idea of writing an introduction to one of my books, but since I know this book will touch on a lot of sensitive subjects, I feel the need to explain to my readers the purpose for writing this story. The concept of a machine that could allow humans to create a separate reality is not only inevitable in the near future—it is, in some ways, present even today. All of life is a dream, whether it is a pleasant one or a straight-up nightmare. We make choices that bring us closer or farther away from our own safety, and the safety of others. We make decisions that bring us closer to truth and love, or closer to lies. This story is a work of fiction, obviously, but the characters in this story could potentially be us. The horrors in this book, the stream of bad choices made, might be worlds away from our standard of ethics and morals, but to some people it may be only one decision away.

I am no advocate to any of the actions in this book, nor do I condone the crimes, addictions, and insecurities of these characters. This book is more of a glimpse into what could be in our world if we don't awaken to the awareness of truth and move towards love. In the same way that drugs don't address the root issues in someone suffering from depression or anxiety, I believe that a virtual reality like the one in this book, although harmless to the humans outside of it, is just as dangerous to the individual and doesn't address the root issue. What is the root issue? I think it's a plethora of lies we've believed about ourselves and others our entire lives. And I believe those lies mold us into the men and women we become. And what is the truth? To me, it's that we are loved unconditionally, and that we are perfect exactly the way we are. You are your perfect self in this moment, and it's effortless.

Enjoy the story and God bless America.

Love,
Benjamin Card

PART ONE: S.T.E.A.M.

———————————————————— ‖

Somewhere in his mind, the desire had been brewing. A pinch of a nerve here, a contraction of a muscle there, making his eyes twitch, his fists clench. Harry Locklin smiled at his wife.

"Yes, dear," he said, stabbing the final chunk of meatloaf on his plate with his fork.

Carla, his wife, smiled amiably back. Behind her cold eyes, he knew that she knew what he was thinking. Everyone knows, in one way or another. Because everyone is guilty of thinking the same thoughts. You can't condemn someone for thinking a thing. But seeing it through, seeing a crime through, changes the course of many lives.

"So you'll wash the dishes before your program?" she asked him for the third time, and it seemed to him like she wanted to get a rise out of him. And why not? She was completely safe.

"I'll wash them, honey." His voice dropped in pitch and vitality. "You can count on it."

So he washed the dishes, pouring himself a glass of whiskey after, and missed the first three minutes of his favorite reality show on television. Sure, the show was recorded on all his devices, but he always liked the idea of watching it as it aired; to be among the first to witness it.

Finally, once he was through, he watched the show silently while Carla checked her emails behind her sunglasses. It made her face look dumb when he would see from the side of his vision his wife's stupid illuminated cheeks as she surfed the web on her dumb glasses. He felt the hot friction of anger sizzle in his veins, making his mind race with hellish scenarios. But he'd do the damn dishes. He'd smash them over her fucking head too, but at least they'd be clean.

Harry's program ended, and he stood from the couch and began to walk over to the garage. That's where they kept S.T.E.A.M.

"Don't forget to wash the whiskey glass too," she said without looking away from her eye-screen.

Harry froze. For a moment he wanted to turn around and toss the glass directly at her glasses. But instead, he took a shallow breath, finished downing the contents of the glass, and marched over to the garage.

"I'll be out in a few minutes," he said without looking her way.

He didn't even bother slamming the door. Why disturb her more? he thought. She'll get what she deserves.

✻

Harry Locklin lay on the bed and attached the clear and silver crown to his head. Sometimes it made his blond hair itch, but as soon as the simulation started up, he wouldn't feel a thing from the outside world. He pressed the ON button near his hip and everything went black.

Welcome back, Harry. Let's get started.

Please imagine your surroundings.

Great. Got it. Now, if you want people there, draw me a mental picture.

Super! You're quite the artist. Have fun. And as always, remove your crown in the simulation to end it. You may now begin.

As the voice faded off, Harry was in his brightly lit kitchen again. *Too goddamn bright if you ask me,* he thought. He went over to his marble counter and picked up the beer opener. With it, he climbed onto the counter and smashed out one of the studio lights above him. The bulb popped into a thousand pieces and rained over his head. He saw his wife turn from the couch, her dumb glasses still on. She removed them eagerly.

"What the fuck do you think you're doing?" she shouted, rising up.

Oh yeah? he thought, tasting the hate and letting it drip into his pumping veins. Let her fucking come over here.

She did, as his imagination destined her to. She marched up to him, and he leaped off the counter.

"You want me to do the dishes?" he said, and sprang his hand hard across her cheek. Carla's head twisted and she spat and moaned.

"You monster!" she cried, bending over the center counter.

Harry walked over to the sink and picked up a dirty plate. It was white and there was gravy residue and some grains of rice on it like bugs on a web.

"You want to remind me to wash this again? After I tell you four hundred fucking times that I'll do it? You wanna scream it at me once more like fucking shock therapy? Here you go, I'll wash it!" Harry swept his dry hands over the plate and the grains of rice landed gracelessly onto the floor. There was some gravy on his palm.

Carla's face looked appalled.

"Not good enough for you?" he ventured. "How's this?"

He swung the plate and it connected with her jaw. A crack sounded, half from the shattered plate and half from Carla's shattered bone. Her bloody head fell against the counter, and she was whimpering with whatever strength was left in her. Harry pulled her up by her shirt and then pushed her to the ground. She fell over like a ragdoll.

"Better?" he said, feeling a bit of guilt but knowing that this was better for him. This got it out of his system. Yes, this was better. This was legal.

He then lowered himself to his knees and lifted the shard of porcelain over his head. He speared downward and the shard pierced Carla's neck. Blood sprang out like a geyser. It felt cold as it sprayed over Harry's face for a second and then subsided to slow gushing pumps of blood that bubbled out of her neck, at the pace of her heartbeat. She used her hands to make an attempt at covering the wound, but there was too much blood, and soon her fingers were lost in a makeover of red sludge. Her eyes were fixed on Harry. Such fear. Such shock. Such disappointment.

"You bitch," he said softly, then dropped the shard. He watched her lying dead for a moment, her arms unmoving, like a snake waiting to pounce. But there was no pounce. Carla was dead.

"All right," he mumbled, and stood. "That's . . . that's enough."

He removed the crown on his head and was immediately transported back to the S.T.E.A.M. bed in his garage. He rose from it quickly, feeling slightly disoriented, as usual. He shook the feeling off and heard the machine say *Goodbye.*

He returned to the living room. Carla was still using her eyeglasses.

"All better?" she said.

"Yes, sweetheart. Any good emails?"

She sighed. "None, baby."

"Too bad," he said.

"Honey, don't forget the whiskey glass."

He lifted it up and smiled. "I'll wash it now, dear."

He walked over to the sink, glancing at the spot on the ground where he'd stabbed her in the neck. He wondered how he might kill her next time, and how soon he'd do it again.

Maybe tomorrow morning before work.

You're tuning into AM 1610, The Cage. Hello caller, what's your name?

James. James Teller.

How old are you, James?

That's classified.

All right. You sound more like James Bond than James Teller. So, as you know, President O'Connor has teamed up with Cloud Nine to help provide S.T.E.A.M. to lower class citizens in thousands of stores and restaurants nationwide. You had some thoughts about this?

Yes. S.T.E.A.M. is ruining this country.

Now come on, James. All you have to do is look at the numbers to know that isn't true. Murder in this country has decreased by 36%, rape decreased by 83%, theft has decreased by 50%! You can't ignore those numbers, James.

No, but you're okay ignoring the rest of the world. All of those crimes have gone up in practically every other country since S.T.E.A.M. was first made public six years ago. The fact is simply this: That when American tourists travel to other countries where they can't "Blow off S.T.E.A.M." they feel entitled to do whatever they want. They—

Well—

—get themselves—

—Well, all right, James—

—into trouble.

Right. All good points. We're going to take another caller now.

2

Michael held the limo door open for his date.

"My God, Sandra, I gotta say again, you look beautiful."

Sandra Brooke smiled. "Thank you . . . again."

The night was cool, with a stillness that made the stir of voices around them soft and sweet. There was a red carpet that led to the Hotel Zion, unwinding up the stairs like a river of Merlot. Hundreds of students were seen through the tall windows of the hotel, which looked into the lower lobby. The place was a palace, with chandeliers lined up on a ceiling that was higher than one's neck could comfortably follow. These were the students of Ferry Grover High. But tonight, they weren't students; they were royalty. In a royal palace. And Sandra Brooke was no exception.

She walked valiantly in her white dress, watching the crowd that was gathered outside slowly turn in awe. Her blonde silky hair almost reflected the flash of photography that sparkled like stars at eye level. When she reached the open lobby doors, the smooth chatter and laughter volleyed around the expansive room, making her heart tickle with joy.

Michael looped his arm through hers, and their fingers knotted together. She smiled inwardly, and, unable to contain the excitement she felt, smiled outwardly as well.

"I think the ballroom is this way," Michael said, leading her through the crowd.

"Okay," Sandra said.

Before they reached the room, two girls popped out of the restroom and shrieked.

"Sandra!" they cried, their arms flailing up as they ran towards her.

"Hey guys," she said smiling.

"You look *sooo* beautiful!" one of them said.

"Yes, just *perfect!*" cried the other.

Sandra giggled. "You two look amazing too!"

They made more small talk before Michael hinted for Sandra to wrap up the conversation. She politely said she had to go and they slipped away into the ballroom. This room was slightly more compact, with a lower ceiling and different chandeliers, but it was just as breathtaking. There were crimson drapes ruffled throughout the walls, and the ceiling was painted with Renaissance-style art.

There were tables dressed in white that spread around the room, leaving a lonely island in the middle which would serve as the dance floor.

They were assigned to Table 12, though they'd made it so they could sit with their closest friends. Elise and Francis, the two girls who'd emerged from the restroom, would not be at that table. They weren't true friends; just the type of friends who glob onto popularity.

Michael pulled back the seat for Sandra, and she sat like a bowing flower, holding her dress at the sides. The group talked, not in turns, and sat in a neat oval. The table cloth hovered just above Sandra's legs, and she brushed the fabric gently with her fingers.

"You like the food?" Michael whispered to her.

They were having grilled chicken with green beans and apple pie for dessert. A small meal, but Sandra wasn't very hungry anyway. Her stomach felt cluttered with twisting knots, some forged in excitement, and some in fear. But she was happy. She looked down at the dinner and smiled at Michael.

"Yes, thank you," she answered.

When the meal was over, the dancing began. The plates of sparse leftovers were deserted and the kids flocked to the center of the room as music began to play. Michael took Sandra's hand, and for the umpteenth time that evening, Sandra felt the cool, uninvited electricity of love. It made her see the world, the room, the people, in a new light. These people are my friends, she thought. Not my enemies. The hate they show is a mask. The same things I love fill them with joy, and the same things I hate fill them with sadness. We're very very alike now.

So they danced. The whole room danced. And no one was left out. Everyone was beautiful that night. Insults and gossip were left behind, in another world. A world not welcome here.

Sandra and Michael spun around the room majestically, their feet taking the form of skates on ice, flying low like birds that flew inches away from the biting oceans, shark infested seas. But the birds were careful. Careful not to cut too low, lest they be drowned and eaten. Just as Sandra was careful, careful but frivolous. It was a carefulness that came naturally, without worry. And it made her confidence swell. I am the most beautiful girl in this room, she thought. And rightfully so. She was. Everyone knew it. Even Michael.

Let me try to read his eyes, she told herself as they danced under the dim lighting. They say . . . they say . . . I see you. I soften myself to really see you. You are so beautiful. I could really love you. Maybe not just tonight, but maybe I could love you for a long, long time.

I hope so, Sandra would answer back. Oh I desperately hope so.

Soon the dancing dwindled down to only a few couples, and then to none as the announcement of Prom King and Queen drew nearer. Sandra had almost forgotten about the event, because, in her mind, she was furthest away from the crown. She never got the attention.

Or even the respect. She wasn't really beautiful. But tonight . . . Tonight. . . .

Tonight was a different story. A story she held the pen to. Why can't I win? she thought, gripping Michael's hand under the tablecloth. Why the hell not?

"The prom King and Queen of Ferry Grover High School is . . ."

She saw the phantom lights drip around the room, lighting the faces of at least three hundred students. The air was just cool enough not to be blazing hot, and her dress felt stuck to her flesh.

"Michael Florence and Sandra Brooke!"

They roared. Her friends, her enemies. God, especially her enemies. They finally saw who she was, who she could be. Such a thing they'd been missing. Such an asset. More than that. She could see it—feel it!—in the primitive power of their applause, in the way they yelled and screamed and hollered. In their wild eyes that shook with remorseful tears. She heard a few *I love yous* and a couple *You deserve its.*

"Come on up, you two!" the female host beckoned, swinging the microphone with inspired energy.

They rose, Michael confidently, and Sandra, despite herself, bashfully. How do I walk up there? she thought as she made her first steps away from the table. The applause never ceased, nor did the hollers of praise. She watched her feet move, like frogs hopping one after the other, she thought, while flashes of photography clapped against the rich crimson carpet, spilling over her amateur feet like wine spilling into a wine glass.

After what seemed like a century, they reached the platform where the host stood waiting. She greeted them as they came near the center of the platform, then spoke.

"Anything you'd like to say to your peers?"

Michael answered first, smiling brightly and kissing Sandra on the cheek. "I'd like to thank all my friends. And Sandra, who brings out the best in me."

The audience roared again, some standing.

"And you?" the host asked Sandra.

Sandra gripped the microphone that was handed to her and noticed how sweaty her hands were. Control yourself, she commanded herself. She also noticed how delicately her fingers trembled, like suicidal teens hesitating at the edge of a cliff.

"I'd like to say," she started, "how grateful I am to be here. And how lucky I am to be standing beside this man. I know it's just a high school thing, but this means so much more to me. I've never felt this much acceptance."

The crowd was silent and observant.

"What I mean is . . . I'll never forget this. Even when I'm older and new memories fog the clarity of the old, I'll remember every breath that left me, every nerve that twitched, and every heartbeat that jumped." Her eyes began to swell with tears. "I . . . I wish I could be here forever. I wish there was no limit."

There's nothing for me back at home. It's what she couldn't bring herself to say.

The host smiled and presented her with a golden tiara. She raised it up and brought it nearer to Sandra. It all happened so fast. The emotions that coursed through her. Such joy and peace and clarity. This was where she belonged.

Then the host stopped, just above her head.

"What's this?" the host inquired. "You already have a crown on your head."

"What?" Sandra said, looking up at the golden crown the host held above her.

"Yeah," Michael said. "You do."

"No I don't," Sandra cried. "Put the crown on."

The host chuckled. "Sandra, check your head."

So she did. She knew. She had forgotten, but right then she knew, even before she touched the top of her head, and felt the cold metal and mechanical wirings, the mechanism that was plopped onto her dumb fat skull. She reached for it, and suddenly the whole scene—the adoring crowd, the beautiful dresses and tuxedos, the lush carpet, the smell of food and perfume, the glistening chandeliers, the sight of Michael—was all gone.

She was back in her room, lying beside her bed. She withdrew the silver crown of S.T.E.A.M. and rose from the white leather bed. Her body shook with spasms of shock and depression. She nearly leaped off the machine and took in the surroundings of her room. She was only gone a few minutes, she realized. She entered her bathroom, which connected to her room. She switched on the light. The brightness burned her eyes for a moment, then they adjusted. She saw herself in the mirror. A fat, pale thing. Fat that pressed against skin and burst out awkwardly; fat that stared back at you sadly, madly, with no solution but to feel obsessively angry. Her face was a mess, like shit pressed into mud. Her eyes too far apart, her cheeks boasting out against each other like disagreeing travelers. Her lips were thin and her teeth uninviting. Her red hair was a net for catching knots. When she even considered beauty again then, the thought was laughable as she gazed into her own eyes.

She clenched her fists together.

"Sandra!" her mother called from another room.

"What!" she shouted impulsively back.

"Prom is starting." Her mother's voice was close to her bedroom door now, no longer shouting. Now it was soft and sympathetic. "You can use my dress. It fits."

Sandra stared at herself in the mirror. The foul, unlovable thing that she was.

"I said I'm not going," she said levelly, gripping the marble sink. "You can't make me."

✳

You're on the air, caller.

This country is being thrown to the wolves.

Who is this?

If we don't abolish S.T.E.A.M. for good, this country is fucked.

You can't curse on the air, sir. Next caller.

3

T he Dylan family was scattered about the house—little Flora Dylan doing homework in her room, Dean Dylan listening to music and chatting online with girls in his room, and Mr. and Mrs. Dylan pulling into the driveway. They had a surprise visitor in their backseat.

"I'll help you out, Dad," Mr. Dylan called as he exited the car.

Grandpa Dylan grunted and lifted his shaky fingers to the door handle. Before he could unlock the thing, Mr. Dylan yanked the door open.

Grandpa shook his head and muttered. "I had it. I had it."

"Alright, Dad, out we go."

Grandpa hated when they treated him like an impotent old geezer. Yes, he was 89; yes, his heart was weak. But he was still the same man, wasn't he? A war hero. A successful businessman. He'd even been interviewed in a few well-known magazines and internet blogs. His business tactics were being taught at several prestigious universities. He could get out of the damned car on his own.

Still, the sun was beaming effectively as he emerged from the back seat. He held the car door like it was a cane and elevated himself to a standing position. He felt his old, loose pores opening up as sweat blinked out of them, and he blinked as well in the blinding light of the April morning.

He trailed behind them as Mr. and Mrs. walked up the small steps to the house. His knees hurt all the time now; they felt like small water balloons waiting to burst at the first miscalculated step.

Once inside, the air was infinitely cooler—like going from Miami to Maine in one swift step. Swift, he almost laughed to himself. That perfectly described his footsteps. Sure, about as swift as bicycling in an earthquake.

"Kids, come say hi to Grandpa!" Mother shouted, dropping her overstuffed purse on the black couch in the living room.

Flora came out, swinging her school binder back and forth.

"Grandpa!" she cried, leaping up as if to have him catch her, but then landing awkwardly back down to the ground, because he couldn't possibly catch her.

"Hey, baby girl," he said, thinking how much older she looked since he last saw her a month ago. She was seven now, a colorful age, and she was a real sweetheart. Not at all like her brother.

"No clue where Dean is," Dad said. "But you know that kid is as elusive as Big Foot. Don't get your feelings hurt if he doesn't come out all night."

I won't, Grandpa thought.

They entered the kitchen and Mr. Dylan pulled up a chair for him. Grandpa sat carefully.

"We have fish for dinner," Mrs. Dylan said. "I hope that's fine."

"It's fine," Grandpa said.

"You want some tomato juice while we wait?" Mr. Dylan said.

Grandpa sighed. "What do you think?"

"Well, Dad, it's good for you. You never have fruits or veggies."

He hated when his son used the word "veggies," like he was a kid.

"I'll have a beer."

"Dad . . ."

"What?"

"You know what."

"I'll have a soda," he said.

"Dad . . . you know the rules here."

"I said I'll have a soda, dammit," he muttered, blinking.

"Dad, you know you can't have a soda."

"Why? Cause it might kill me? Who goddamn cares? I'm 89 years old. What do I have to watch out for?"

"Dad, I'll get you a ginger ale."

"All right," he said, nodding.

Mr. Dylan brought him a ginger ale can and opened it for him. Mrs. was finishing up cooking. Then Mr. went to the bathroom. And Mrs. went over to call her son in for dinner. Grandpa was alone with Flora. She was sitting on the stool and smiling at him, her pencil tapping against her notebook.

"What are you working on there?" he asked.

"School assignment. For science."

"Hmm," he mumbled.

He couldn't deny what was on his mind. He hadn't had a drink in a week. That may not seem long to some people, but when you've been drinking heavily since the age of 14, a week can feel like a lifetime. And he knew he couldn't sneak in a beer. His family would stop him before he finished half a can. And . . . he had to face it: his heart and his liver were both weak. It wasn't a good idea. But . . .

But . . . S.T.E.A.M. That's what was on his mind. They had a machine in the laundry room, right beside the kitchen. He had time. It only took a minute and it would feel like an hour to him. It might satisfy for the time being. Hell, he deserved it didn't he?

He rose weakly, while Flora concentrated on her homework. He walked over to the laundry room. It was humid in there, and smelled of detergent and linen. He saw the S.T.E.A.M. pressed into the corner of the wall, behind a rack of clothes hangers. He moved there as quickly as he could and lay down. Even if he only had 20 seconds, in the world of S.T.E.A.M. that would translate to at least 20 minutes.

He put on the crown and closed his eyes.

Welcome, guest. Let's get started.

Please imagine your surroundings.

Only one thing was on his mind.

Great. Got it. Now, if you want people there, draw me a mental picture.

He wanted no one there.

Super! Just you then. Have fun. And as always, remove your crown in the simulation to end it. You may now begin.

✻

Grandpa opened his eyes. He was in a giant room. Like a wine cellar. But it wasn't filled with just wine. Each rack had different assortments of whiskey, gin, vodka, rum, tequila, every type of liquor you could imagine. There was beer, too. He laughed and lifted his arms. He felt young again, too. Gone was the weakness in his bones, and gone was the pain in his knees and feet and the difficulty to breathe. He ran over to the whiskey and grabbed a random bottle. It was a brand of cinnamon whiskey. That would do just fine. He didn't have time to be picky. He twisted open the bottle and sucked on it like a pacifier. The warm liquor burned beautifully down his throat. He took at least five large gulps and then tossed the bottle. It smashed against the wall. He laughed hysterically, running up to the collection of rum bottles. He didn't really love rum, but today he would have it all. He took a shot of clear rum and gagged a little. This just made him laugh more.

The room he was in looked old and had stone walls. He had always been fascinated by the style of the early 1900s, and knew that that had been in his mind when S.T.E.A.M. created this paradise for him.

He went over to the gin and took a few swigs of that. There was a smooth, minty flavor to it. He started to feel the sweet wooziness of intoxication and shouted randomly with joy. Finally! No one to bother him. No rules. No danger. Just pure bliss!

He tossed at least ten bottles in the air just for the heck of it, watching them smash against the floor like hail. He spun around the room with a bottle of tequila, dancing with it, humming a melody he'd learned in the war. He took a swig of that and tossed it aside.

"I think I'll have some of . . . you!" he announced as he picked up a bottle of vodka. This he chugged grotesquely, not caring about the rancid flavor and the disgust he felt. He was wallowing in it and it was all okay.

He felt drunk. Gloriously drunk. Like his college years. He wished he'd imagined a young beautiful woman in here with him too, but it was too late for that. He didn't have much time left, he knew. Once his son found out he was here, he'd be snapped back to a sober, dull reality.

He took a seat on a wooden bench and opened a new bottle of whiskey. He drank a little and thought about his life. Why was it that every pleasurable thing was bad for you? And vice versa. Was this God's way of tormenting humans, or teaching them? It didn't matter. When they invented S.T.E.A.M., they figured out a way to outsmart God. Right and wrong didn't matter anymore, at least not for most people. All that mattered now was avoiding bad consequences. And this alternate reality made it possible to do just that.

He raised the whiskey bottle to his lips. This time, he tried to really focus on the flavor. He wanted to really savor it. He looked at the brown liquid and watched it swirl as he rotated the bottle in a circular motion. Then he took a small pool of whiskey in his mouth and kept it there. He felt it burn slightly, the potent flavor of the liquor coming and going while his tongue became a little numb. It tasted like the best parts of history. It tasted like what it meant to live in the world as a man. It tasted real. And solid. He swallowed and felt the warm whiskey go down like a bullet being shot out from a pistol. It settled in his stomach and he grinned. *They can't stop me,* he thought.

But then they did. He was pulled away from his oasis as fast as he'd arrived, and the next thing he knew, his son was standing over him, silver crown in hand, looking down at him with anger.

"Dad!" he shouted. "How could you?"

Grandpa felt sober again. It was a strange feeling to have all that intoxication flushed out of your mind in an instant. He sat up, struggling to do so.

"I was only gone a minute."

"Did you . . . did you do what I think you did?"

He considered lying about it, but he knew they wouldn't believe him. And hell, why should he have to lie anyway? This wasn't real. There were no consequences here. At least, no consequences one could see. The consequences, though Grandpa didn't realize, ran deep to the core of the heart and what it wanted. What it needed. That would never go away, even in the real world.

"Yes!" Grandpa shouted. "I did! I did it! Who cares? Now go serve me that rancid fish!"

AM 16.10! Your place for the best news in technology. Cloud Nine has introduced TagBonds, a new update for the S.T.E.A.M. software that allows you to sync with up to six other users to create a world of your own. Sounds pretty promising. And the best part? The update is absolutely free! Rejoice, S.T.E.A.M. users. This ought to change the whole game! Anyway, let's get our next caller on the line. What's your name?

James Teller.

. . . Wait. Is this the same guy from yesterday? How are you getting through the lines so easily?

Don't worry about that. Let's talk TagBonds.

Fine, sir. What's your concern this time?

I'm concerned with the repercussions that are sure to come from this. It's bad enough to have the freedom to do any crime you want. But to have others witnessing it now? To have . . . accomplices? It's going to affect the real world. People will see. The hatred will seep out of the confines of the machine.

Okay, Negative Nancy. Is that all?

No, it's not all.

Well I've heard enough. Next caller.

4

Eddie Loffman kept rolling his eyes in a way that only barely strained them. But in some cases, like when Casey would lean over her desk to grab something from her book bag, he craned his neck in her direction without shame, watching the small slit of shadow that just atomically revealed her white bra. When she rose her frame up again, sometimes glancing his way skeptically, Eddie would dart his attention to the assignment on his desk. Which, unfortunately for him, was an Algebra assignment. He thought he had a better chance of actually undressing Casey with his eyes than he had of solving some of these math problems.

"Creep," a boy behind him said, and coughed to mask the word.

Some other boys—and girls—laughed. Eddie felt himself blushing.

"Now," said Mrs. Harriot, the teacher. "Does this sound like the peace and quiet I asked for at the beginning of class?"

One of the students across the room must've mumbled something funny, though Eddie didn't hear it, because a few other kids in his vicinity chuckled.

"I said quiet!" she yelled. Mrs. Harriot was a slightly large woman in her early forties; though she had really nice eyes and a nice face overall. She combed her black hair with her fingers and sat down again, the leather rolling chair making a soft noise of leather stretching as she did.

Eddie tried to concentrate on his school work, but the image of Casey's bra kept resurfacing in his mind. It played back like a looping image, and in his imagination, he had the freedom to make her do other things. He could undress her with his mind, or make her bend over, with her ass reaching out, calling his name. *Eddie, come get me, Eddie. Take it, Eddie. Why not, Eddie? Oh Eddie!*

He sighed and sat up straighter, surveying the room to make sure nobody noticed that he was getting aroused. He could see some trees and clouds out the long window that took up the entire west wall of the room. The room was almost dead quiet now, the kids actually working. *Why can't I focus?* wondered Eddie. He knew what could make this go away, but it was impossible. The only S.T.E.A.M. machine available was in the teacher's lounge, and S.T.E.A.M. was illegal to anyone under the age of 18. But . . . perhaps he could still get to it. God, it would be so nice. To have Casey to himself for just an hour. All to himself. To take her thick blonde hair in his hands and feel her soft white flesh against his. To lift her school dress up over her ass and to—

"Quiet!" Mrs. Harriot said again as some students chuckled.

Eddie couldn't take it. He had to get in there. He didn't know how, but he had to try. What's the worst that would happen? He might be suspended for a couple days, but that's about it. This was worth it. To have sex with Casey was definitely worth it.

He hated even speaking aloud in class. The attention was always something that stole directly from his confidence. But he spoke out anyway, knowing that if he didn't, he might completely lose his mind.

"Mrs. Harriot," he said, shooting his arm up awkwardly. "I need to use the restroom."

She looked at him strangely, and shrugged, gesturing for him to go. As if he didn't need to ask permission. But of course he had to ask. She enforced the rule that they all had to ask. Some of the students chuckled as he got up.

Stupid bitch, Eddie thought. *Don't treat me like some idiot. I asked because you always yell at us to ask. And now you make me out to be an idiot because I do what you say? Dumb fucking fat bitch.*

He wasn't even sure why he was so angry, or really what about, but he felt his anger swell with each calculated step, until he reached the door and yanked it open.

It was quiet out in the hall. He knew where the teacher's lounge was, but didn't have a key to get in. He would have to wait for someone to come out. And once in, how would he convince whoever else was in there that he belonged? *I just have to act confident,* he told himself. *Act like I do belong.*

He passed the last row of lockers before reaching the door that said LOUNGE over it. He waited by the drinking fountain, pretending to take a sip every few seconds. A security guard passed by almost as soon as he got there, but for some reason he didn't see Eddie.

Eddie waited anxiously. Finally, after about three minutes, a woman came out. It was the drama teacher, Miss Ferguson. She straightened out her skirt; Eddie caught the door and—with as much confidence as he could muster—walked in. There was no one else in there! Eddie laughed lowly and walked quickly over to the back room, where S.T.E.A.M. was, in the dark. He left the light off and sat inside. He was afraid that he would need a password, but there was none. The machine started up automatically. He donned the crown and closed his eyes.

✳

He was in the classroom again. He seemed to land into the room on his feet like someone coming off a swing set. He looked around nervously, thinking that everything looked exactly how he'd left it. This was, after all, his first time ever using S.T.E.A.M. He wasn't exactly sure how it worked. Some high schools had a mandatory "S.T.E.A.M. Ethics" course, but not his.

He began to walk slowly to where his desk was. Yes . . . everything looked eerily similar. Was his memory that precise? That he could recall everything exactly as it was in reality? Maybe not. Maybe it was a deeper scientific thing in the subconscious that helped him remember. Either way, everything looked identical. He couldn't point out one difference. Except, of course, that here, nobody was looking at him funny as he walked to his desk. Everyone just sat still. Including Casey. She looked beautiful. Eddie wondered if he could just crouch down in front of her. What would happen? Would she react at all?

He stood in front of her, feeling his heart beat like a bullet in his chest, afraid that maybe this *wasn't* S.T.E.A.M. after all. Maybe he'd messed the process up and somehow ended up back in class.

No. That wasn't possible. He could tell by the vacant look in their eyes that these people weren't real.

He crouched down, gripping the edge of the wooden desk. She looked into his eyes. Her eyes were like a blue flame.

"Casey," Eddie whispered.

Everything in the room was silent. Eddie half-expected to hear his teacher call him out from behind. But nobody said a word.

"Eddie," Casey said, smiling.

Eddie felt his nerves shiver, and his heart seemed to punch out his chest.

He extended his arm and took her hand in his. They held hands over her math text book. *But why isn't she saying a word?* he wondered. Wasn't this thing supposed to simulate personalities as well? Why was everyone acting like robots? Maybe he screwed up somewhere along the process. The machine was supposed to reenact the personalities you enable it to from your subconscious. Maybe—since he only knew his classmates as bullies who only had cruel things to say—his subconscious blanked out their personalities altogether. That somehow made sense to him. Fine, he thought. I'll just have to make do with these robots then. Maybe it would be easier this way.

"Casey," he whispered again, leaning into her. He kissed her lips. They felt so real; they *were* real. This was her, he convinced himself. Feeling himself getting aroused again, he stood up in a jerking motion and pushed her desk sideways. She didn't seem too startled, only looked up at him with blank eyes. Eddie pulled her up and she obediently stood in front of him. No one else in the class muttered a word. He felt rushed all of a sudden. He didn't know how long time in S.T.E.A.M. translated in real life, so he was afraid of being pulled away too soon. Before he could . . .

He suddenly bent Casey over on the desk and began tugging at her skirt. It came down rather easily, revealing her white panties. He then took down his own pants. He was for a second amazed at how real the arousal felt, how completely erect he was. But his attention was diverted quickly from that when he saw Casey's milk-white cheeks bent over like that. He pulled her panties off almost violently, and took no caution to enter her. *That blonde hair is Casey's blonde hair,* he thought. *I'm going to fuck Casey.* He began thrusting into her. Over and over. Moaning uncontrollably.

He didn't care that the entire class watched.

✳

When he was finished with her (it didn't take long. He couldn't seem to hold it in; and honestly didn't try to), he stepped away from her. Feeling shame for a moment, he pulled up his pants hastily. He looked around, his eyes darting around the room like they were locking onto missiles. The peering eyes of his peers seemed just as dangerous to him. Maybe even more so, because he felt a little like dying right then. But these eyes wouldn't kill him. They just continued staring at him blankly. Blankly. Not smiling nor frowning. Just even lips, not parted. Eyes that said they could see but could not tell. Eddie felt mad inside.

"Stop looking at me!" he cried. "She isn't real! I didn't do anything wrong. This is legal! Everyone does it!"

He walked up to Mrs. Harriot and slapped her across the face. "Especially you!" he shouted. "I said stop staring!"

He felt so dirty and foolish. He didn't know why. He knew that all of this was only a simulation; as innocent as the times he would fantasize about Casey in his mind.

Nobody was really being affected. So why did this bother him so much?

He thought he knew the answer, but he pushed it away because he was afraid. And just as he pushed the thought away, he reached out his arms and pushed the crown away, too.

Instantly, he was brought back to the darkness of the teacher's lounge. The room felt colder than he remembered, and he could hear a rumbling coming from the air vent above him too. Something he hadn't noticed earlier. He looked at his watch. He'd only been in there three minutes. That was good. There was still time to get to class without anyone noticing.

He left the lounge and carefully looked around in the halls. There was nobody around. He walked at an awkward pace, hearing his shoes squeak over the freshly-swept tiled floor. As he reached his classroom, he peered into the window on the door. He could see his teacher still sitting at her desk, grading some papers. Eddie cleared his mind, and walked in.

Most of the students were staring at him. Casey was not. He almost felt like she knew what he'd done. He reached his seat and dropped his weak hands on the desk. The room was quiet. He imagined that he was still in S.T.E.A.M. Everything about the atmosphere felt the same. Except the stares weren't as heavy. They came and flitted away. And these stares weren't vacant. They carried questions. Casey, my Casey, he thought. Why couldn't he touch her in real life?

Because that's illegal, the voice of reason said within him.

But what I did in that machine . . . . That was okay, wasn't it? Of course it was.

Well, let's think, the voice chanted. *If Casey knew what you did, if she knew every dirty detail, do you think* she'd *think it was "okay?"*

Well what difference does that make? Eddie thought. She never had to know. Nobody had to know. This was as private as masturbation. Casey, for instance, didn't have to know that he'd pleasured himself to her pictures online about a hundred times in the past, did she? No. That was a man's private life. And it wasn't shameful, Eddie reminded himself. Everyone was guilty for doing it. So what did this matter? S.T.E.A.M. was only a better form of what'd he'd already been doing for a long time.

So tell her, the voice, malignant and officious as it was, whispered to him.

"I don't have to tell her a damn thing," Eddie spoke, so low that he was positive no one could hear.

He suddenly became astute to the noises around him. He heard the tapping of pencils, the flurry of papers being shuffled, the thump of book bags being dropped, zippers being opened, desks being shifted—making the sound of elephant trunks. He heard coughs and sighs, sneezes and burps. He saw Mrs. Harriot yawn and he wanted to slam him fist into her mouth. Make her already-bulging eyes roll out of their sockets. And Casey

. . . to Casey, he wanted to do what he'd already done just minutes ago.

"I want to fuck her," he whispered again, making sure especially now that nobody could hear him.

His wrists twitched, and he sat up straighter. He felt arousal surfacing again, but this time he couldn't do anything about it. Think of something else. Think of anything else. The sounds around you. Or think of punching that fat bitch Mrs. Harriot again. Just don't think *that!*

He hadn't noticed how much time had passed, but soon enough the bell rang. It cried while the students hoisted their bags and belongings. Eddie just sat frozen, unable to do anything but watch as Casey slung her bag over her shoulder and rose to leave. Most of the students had gone by the time she reached the door. She tucked a strand of her blonde hair behind her ear, and blinked as she disappeared behind the open door. Eddie was the last one in the room, and Mrs. Harriot kept watching him.

Finally, Eddie swallowed and looked at his teacher.

She smiled and aimed those bulging eyes at him. "You know," she said. "If you like her so much, you should just tell Casey what you think about her."

Eddie blinked and clutched his book bag and brought it close to his chest.

"What's the worst that could happen?"

He rose quickly and left the room without saying a word.

✳

The Cage. What's on your mind, caller?

Freedom.

James . . . God dammit. Why this station? There are plenty of other stations you can hack and torment. Why this one?

Freedom.

I'm tired of this. You're going to force this station to stop taking callers altogether.

You could never do that.

What do you want? I don't control S.T.E.A.M. I'm just a user like everybody else.

How innocent of you.

We'll stop taking callers. All right? Will that make you happy, you little asshole?

Then I'll just take over the whole damn radio. I'm giving America one last chance. In just about—

—Is that a threat, you prick?

It's what I'm doing. Not a threat so much as an appointment.

And what's gonna happen then?

I'll get my way, either way.

You wanna know something, James? I pictured you last night in my S.T.E.A.M. unit. I only had your voice to go by, but I kept the room dark and your voice was all I needed. And you want to know what I did? Huh, you fucking prick? I bashed your skull in with a hammer! I felt your brain catch the blow of my fucking hammer head, James! I fucking—what? Hey! What the hell are you doing—! GET OFF ME!

5

Amy Ryan looked at her husband who was napping on their pleather couch, his legs hanging off the tattered arm of the furniture, which was cut open and revealed blooming clusters of cotton and foam.

She grunted and moved over to him. Slapping his leg, he snapped awake.

"What!" he roared.

"What?" she screeched. *"What?* Whatta you think, huh? The paper's ova there by the TV, you haven't even looked in it!"

The man, his name was Ryan (so his full name was Ryan Dallas Ryan), propped himself up on his elbows.

"I was tired," he said, looking around to find the paper.

" 'Tired,' " she said. " 'Tired.' Well God forbid you're tired, since you can't even—"

"Don't *fucking* start, Amy. Don't fucking start."

He got up and snatched the newspaper. It was still called a newspaper, but in these days the newspaper was made of some kind of plastic and had moving pictures and videos in it. It was all done through some wireless connection which was limited to only the current day's paper, which made it fairly cheap to subscribe to. Definitely cheaper, at least, than buying or renting a computer of their own. The Ryan family didn't have much money. No, that wasn't the truth. They didn't have more than a few bucks to their name. They owned their small two bedroom house thanks to Amy's grandmother who left the house for her in her will. Before that she and Ryan had been renting out a dingy apartment in Camden that flaunted the unique view of a darkened, piss-laden alley.

"We need money, Ryan," Amy said.

"Don't you fucking think I know that?" Ryan fired back. "And where's your job, huh?"

"I'm trying, Ryan. I'm trying. I've applied to four places today. That restaurant down by Greene."

"All right. I'll get it done, babe."

"Good," she said, dropping her hands from her hips.

"Wait—what restaurant? Muggy's Bistro?"

"Yeah, so what?"

"Nothin'. Don't they have S.T.E.A.M.?"

Amy moved over to the couch, the floor creaking beneath her feet as she went, and snatched the newspaper from Ryan's hand.

"They have two. So?" she said. "Why does that matter? They charge."

"I know, I know . . ." he started, then shook his head. "I don't know. I just thought . . . . Maybe that's what we need. It might inspire us. You know, like a vacation." He flinched after he said this, expecting her to lash out at him again. But, to his surprise, she was silent.

When he looked at her, her eyes seemed to reach inward, at herself.

"We got enough?" she asked.

"Yes," Ryan said, sounding excited. "We'll be tight once we get back, but that would just motivate us to find work faster."

She was nodding, looking at the shoddy environment around her. The small television set, the fake wood floor, the noisy air conditioner. Yes, they needed this. A vacation would be good for them. And in the alternate reality of S.T.E.A.M., half an hour would feel like a four day vacation!

"Would we get to go togetha?"

"Yes," he said, moving to the kitchen and opening a drawer beside the sink where their last few dollars were hidden. "They've updated the new software on all S.T.E.A.M. units in the county. We can link up if we both use the same passcode."

She was quiet for a moment, then nodded. "Okay," she said.

"What's wrong?"

"Nothing," she said. "Just thinkin' if we should go to Hawaii or Cancun."

Ryan smiled and raised their last twenty-dollar bill to her. "Why not both?"

✻

They arrived at Muggy's less than an hour later. The bus ride there was hot and crowded. Everyone seemed preoccupied in their own wicked imaginings. As the bus turned and braked, the mass of sweaty passengers swayed and slumped forward, like the whole thing was choreographed. Amy looked out the window and saw Muggy's Bistro—the rusty yellow letters were bolted just below the roof of the small building, some of the letters in 'Bistro' were crooked. When the bus stopped about a block away from the establishment, Ryan and Amy paid and hopped off.

They walked in a hurry, feeling the enchantment of a vacation just at arm's reach.

"A cruise!" Amy announced as they speed-walked down the street.

"Yeah!" said Ryan. "All you can eat—"

"Swimming pools!"

"Presidential Family Suite!"

They reached and entered Muggy's Bistro. There were elegant dining tables lining both sides of the small restaurant, and a small bar in the back of the room. Chandeliers hung classically above the guests who were sitting, talking quietly, all dressed casually, and some eating and drinking. At the far left of the room, they could see the wooden sign above that read S.T.E.A.M. SERVICES. There was a crimson veil that hid the small room in back, and Ryan and Amy made their way there quickly and discreetly. As they passed the different families that ate, Amy felt a bit of jealousy. Though Muggy's wasn't a very expensive dining place, it wasn't the type of place they could just decide to go to whenever they pleased. This troubled her, and she wondered if they would always have to settle for attaining wealth only by the limited faculties that S.T.E.A.M. supported.

Ryan swung the veil aside. One of the machines was vacant, but one was occupied.

"Now what?" Amy asked.

"What do you mean? We wait. Do we have a choice?"

So they waited about ten minutes before a man who appeared to be in his early forties, wearing a Hawaiian shirt and khaki shorts emerged from the machine. His brown hair was thin and stuck to the sweat on his forehead. When he saw the Ryans, his eyes looked hazy and shaky, like he hadn't expected to encounter anyone so soon after returning to reality. He stood promptly and left the room without a word.

"Guess we're up," Ryan said, taking the bed that the man had been occupying.

"Guess so," Amy said, taking the other.

They both lay horizontal, adjusting the crown on their heads.

"Ready, babe?" Ryan said.

"Ready. Now what?" It had been months since her last S.T.E.A.M. trip. And she had never been on a trip with someone else. The linked machines were a new update.

"Okay, I'll design the cruise ship," Ryan said. "You don't have to worry about that. You just focus on the things *on* the cruise that you want. And the people."

"Got it," she said, feeling slightly nervous and not knowing why.

Welcome, guests. Let's get started.

Please imagine your surroundings.

A moment passed and Amy wondered what exactly her husband was thinking.

Great. Got it. Now, if you want people there, aside from your link buddy, draw me a mental picture.

This was Amy's job, and she forced her mind to conjure up the ideal people.

Splendid! Got it all down. Have fun. And as always, remove your crown in the simulation to end it. You may now begin.

The first thing that Amy noticed was the sound of the ocean crashing against the heavy body of the ship. Then she felt the wind; pulsing violently against her cheeks, making her t-shirt flap in the wind like a raised flag. She opened her eyes and the light was blinding. Even before she fully saw her surroundings, she felt a wave of peace spill over her. She felt something warm over her hand, and when she turned to look, she saw Ryan lying on a beach chair beside her, his hand folded over her own.

"We made it," he said, relief in his words.

Though there was never any real danger involved, Amy felt that a trip to the S.T.E.A.M. dimension was sometimes frightening in the sense that, one never knew for sure if his mind would betray him. So there was a sense of floating through a timeless space, almost as in teleportation, where every cell of the human anatomy breaks apart and you hope—and pray—that the pieces will come together all right on the other side.

It was like that now, but so far. Amy seemed pleased with her surroundings: the people on deck spread thin, some leaning on the railing, watching the endless ocean peel layer upon layer of sparkling salt water, and some lying down, letting the sun whisper its poetry over their skin. There were no children that Amy could see; maybe because she always felt irritated by children in these types of places.

"Well?" Ryan said smiling.

"It's spectacular," she said.

"Shall we go exploring? Find our room?"

"Where is our room?" she asked.

"Let's see." Ryan fished out a laminated card from his pocket. On the back it said Riviera 211.

So they walked in the warm breeze, lacing their fingers together and swinging their arms playfully. First, they stopped at the bar to get two strawberry Daiquiris. The bartender was a large, jittery man with chest hairs protruding from his v-neck shirt and his black hair in a ponytail. They took their drinks with them and continued walking.

Amy felt a peace that had been absent in her life for years. Why hadn't they done this before? Money, of course, had thwarted their attempts of having a vacation like this in the *real* world. But in here, it was affordable and just as beautiful—if not more so!

Once inside the cruise ship, Ryan and Amy marveled at the subtle luxury of the place. There were dozens of stores, like in a mall, that sold everything from fine jewelry to snow globes to sex toys. And at the far center were the two large elevators that could be seen through a glass exterior that shuttled the elevators down like bubbles traveling through a syringe. They went a few floors down to the Riviera deck, which was much stuffier and smaller than the Lido deck, but just as luxurious.

When they got to their room, Ryan scanned the card at the door and a little green light lit up. He pushed the handle down and the heavy door opened. The room was a nice size, maybe about three-hundred square feet.

"Our clothes are here!" Amy proclaimed, running to the luggage that was stacked over their king size bed.

"Yeah, baby," Ryan said. "I made sure of it."

"Oh, babe," she said, feeling the tickle of tears forming under her skin.

"Told you this would be perfect," he said, unzipping his black bag and fishing out a white shirt that was very wrinkled.

"Oh it is. It *is*."

"Wanna shower with me before dinner?" he said, smiling softly at her.

She smiled back and nodded.

Ryan replaced the wrinkly shirt on the small table in the room and smoothed it out with his hands. Then he turned with as much of a romantic stride as he could muster into his walk and grabbed Amy by the arms.

"I love you, baby," he said, his eyes like two dark moons in the room.

We're here, Amy thought, but we're not here. How real is this? Why isn't this as real as real life? It sure did have all the qualities of life. All the senses and all the emotions. This was her husband, as far as she could tell.

"I love you too, Ryan," she said.

They undressed and stepped into the fairly small, rectangular shower. The water came out in pulsing spurts at first, then gushed out smoothly. It was cold for a second and they both laughed, jumping to the side and grabbing each other's naked bodies.

"This is our fantasy," Ryan said, his voice echoing in the small space of the bathroom. "You'd think we would remember to use hot water in our subconscious."

Amy laughed at that, but then she thought, maybe these small imperfections *are* what make a trip perfect. Those are the quirky things you remembered when you got back home. So maybe this, all of it, from the musty hallways in the deck to the dysfunctional showerhead, was in its own way perfect. All she knew was that she felt absolutely happy. She had forgotten what the feeling felt like. But here it was. And she tried to neglect the thought—the reality—that it would be over soon.

After their shower, they got dressed for their first formal dinner on the ship. Amy wore a white dress that had a black trim outlining the hem of the dress and the collar. She let her hair down and, after drying it, curled it. Her brown curly hair, by the time they were ready to go, looked as elegant as a flower arrangement. Ryan, of course, was done getting ready way before her. But he seemed content lying on the bed watching a program on the television. It was a program that showed the different activities one could do on the cruise.

"Each night is Comedy Night at the Houston Lounge. Special guest Fabio Vazquez followed by headliner Daniel Brown Jr. And grab your friends for Karaoke right after at 11."

"I'm ready," Amy announced, turning excitedly to her husband.

"Oh baby," he said, marveling at her beauty. "Let's forget dinner. I think I wanna undress you again right now."

She laughed, blushing. "Shut up!"

"All right, all right, let's get going. I just have a feeling we'll be having your favorite dish tonight." He smirked.

"You didn't," she said giggling.

"I did!" he said. "Fettuchini Alfredo with shrimp and a side of French Onion soup!"

✳

But they never got that dinner. They were yanked away. That's the only way Amy could describe the feeling.

Yanked. Like a child from her mother. It happened just as they were entering The Grande Dining Room. She could see the lights; smell the fresh coffee and the aroma of sauces permeating the air. She could hear the happy chatter moving in the room like sun-speckled waves crashing on the shore.

Then. *Then.*

Yanked.

"No," was all she could mutter. She was lying in the machine, her cold metal crown scratching on her skull. "What happened?"

Ryan, who she could see still lying there, dumb-founded, craned his neck to her.

"What happened?" he said as well.

"I don't know," she said. "We're back too soon." She began to shout. "We're back too soon! It should have been four days! Four days! We're back too-"

"Baby, calm down," Ryan said. "We'll go back. Let me find a manager."

Ryan stood and looked at the machine. It was completely off. He checked the outlet but it was still plugged in.

"I'll . . . I'll get the manager," he said again. He passed through the curtain that separated the restaurant from the room and Amy waited for him to return. It only took a minute.

Ryan returned with a man dressed in a black suit. His hair was gelled to the side and his eyebrows were bushy. He smiled with fat lips.

"Like I told your husband," he said to her. "We're working on the issue now. It seems to be happening all around this part of the city. I assure you it's nothing serious. I can refund you the money you lost. A full refund."

Amy was stunned. She sat there immobile, watching her husband and then the man in suit.

"How . . ." she started. "How long will it take?"

The man pursed his lips. Those fat lips. "I'm not sure, ma'am. I really can't say. I assure you it's nothing serious. If you want to leave your name and number, we can call you as soon as it's up and running again. I'm very sorry about the inconvenience."

"Yes," Amy said. "It is an inconvenience."

"Shall I write down . . ." the man started hesitantly.

"Yes," she said. "Take down our number."

"I'm sorry, baby," Ryan said. "We'll come back once it's running."

"Sure," she said, still feeling dazed. They'd gone from the gutter of New Jersey to paradise and back. So soon. Too soon.

Ryan helped his wife out of the S.T.E.A.M. bed and they followed the manager out of the room. The restaurant was still packed. Some of the people watched as they emerged from the curtained back room. After the manager refunded them their money, they made their way through the restaurant.

"Don't worry," Ryan said again. "I'm sure it won't take long. I'll fill out some applications while we're waiting. I got inspired by that trip, even if it was cut short."

She was practically being pulled out by her husband, because her feet didn't seem to move on their own. Yanked.

Then she turned and saw a couple eating. The woman was dressed in a pink dress. Her hair was in curls, as Amy's had been. And she was eating . . .

Fettuchini Alfredo with shrimp.

Amy yanked (*yanked!*) her arm free from Ryan's grip and flung the woman's pasta dish to the ground.

The woman looked appalled as they both ran out of the restaurant into the urban streets of New Jersey.

✳

Next caller.

Time's running out. Can you feel it?

No, James. No, I don't feel a thing. Let me do my job, James. Leave me alone today, James. Just today. The police are looking for you, you know. They're out there now, listening to this, and looking for you. They think you're responsible for the shutdown in Jersey.

They won't find me.

Don't do this, James. You can still stop this. Let us live in peace.

Peace? You know nothing about peace. I've seen what S.T.E.A.M. can do to the mind. It happened to me.

Please, James. We're happy this way. End it.

No . . . I'm sorry, friend. Not yet.

Damn you to hell, James.

6

Irene Foster stepped off the sidewalk and watched a car roll past her. The car drove by her so quickly that it raised a small wave of rain water from the ground. Irene stomped back and the wave just missed her, subsiding on the curb and making her feet look like two islands as the murky water gathered around them. She looked up and saw the sun setting just behind a stack of corporate buildings.

It was Christmas Eve. She saw the streets filled with cars that were filled with gifts. She could see the gifts piled in some of the cars; shopping bags protruding like gelled-up hair, some white and some black and some yellow or brown. There were a lot of last-minute shoppers in New York. But she wasn't in the streets for shopping.

"Excuse me, miss," a young voice said from behind her.

Irene turned around. There was a young man and he was wearing a brown coat and jeans. His brown boots seemed too big for him.

"Yes?" Irene said.

"I was wondering if you knew where I could find the nearest S.T.E.A.M. unit."

Irene tried to speak, but her words seemed caught in her throat.

The man smiled jovially. "Have you committed a crime, girl?"

"What?" Irene asked, appalled. "What are you talking about?"

James's smile faded. "You look distressed. I thought maybe you'd done a crime recently in S.T.E.A.M."

"Well that's a stupid assumption. I've never used S.T.E.A.M."

"You haven't?" The boy seemed impressed by this. "How old are you?"

"Nineteen."

"Then you're legal. You've had a whole year to use it and you haven't?"

"No," she said.

"Why not?"

"I don't know. I don't like it."

The boy smiled again, his shoulders relaxed. "Neither do I. But I don't think it'll be around for much longer."

They were quiet a second. "Are you through asking me questions?"

His smile expanded more, revealing his glossy gums. "You bet."

He waved her off and she passed him.

After she'd gone for about a block, she turned back to see if he was still standing there. She for some reason expected that he was. And he was. His hands were in his pockets, and he was the size of a light bulb now. And he still seemed to be smiling.

✳

Irene made it to a park with an unattended playground and different batches of trees that had been planted there recently, manually. The swings had rust on them and small pools of water were on the bottom of the two yellow slides. There was a bench with an ad for a skin cleanser, but the bench looked wet too.

Irene saw a doughnut shop across the park and decided to grab some coffee.

As she entered, she could smell the thick odor of sugar and coffee stuffed in the small, warm room. She ordered an espresso and chatted with the cashier for a while. He was an older man in his late thirties. He said his name was Hal.

"What's that room back there?" Irene asked him, still waiting for her cup to cool down.

The man didn't have to look back. "That's our S.T.E.A.M. room."

The room looked like a doorless closet. There was no sign or anything to advertise the room, but Irene then noticed the sticker on the menu that said *"Blow off some S.T.E.A.M. Ask us where!"*

"Does it work?"

"Sure," he said.

"Do you use it?" Irene asked.

"Sure," he said. "On my breaks."

Irene tried to imagine what this man would do in there. Murder his boss. Rape his sister. Rob the bank. They were all plausible evils that could be done with no consequences, and it made her sick to her stomach.

"Want to give it a whirl?" the man said.

Irene looked at him. "Oh, I've never used it."

"It's not hard. It's easy. Like going to sleep and waking up again."

She shrugged and took a sip of her coffee, which was cooler now. "I don't think there's anything I'd want to do."

"Nothing at all?"

"I don't think so."

"You can do anything you want."

"I know."

"Doesn't have to be a bad thing."

She paused. She hadn't considered that. But still, she couldn't think of a thing.

"I still don't know."

The man leaned on the counter. He cleared his throat. "You know, I've seen about three hundred people come in here and use that thing since we installed it just a month ago. You wanna know what I've seen in all of those people?"

Irene instinctively inched closer to the counter. "What?"

"Squeezing in. Holding in. Like they've got a bladder problem. I see it in their shaking eyes and their tight little walk. It's like they see S.T.E.A.M. the same as taking a crap. If they didn't have access to it, they'd take a shit out in the streets. And that means doing something awful. So, Irene, you never have to take a crap?"

Irene had to giggle at that. "Sure, even pretty girls like me have to do that. But not the crap you're talking about. You know, there was a time when people didn't even know that this kind of . . . crap . . . even existed. Call me crazy but I think the world was better off that way."

"Hmm," Hal said.

Irene didn't like the way he was looking at her. His smile was flirtatious and his eyes seemed to be saying *I want to fuck you. And I probably will as soon as you get out of here.*

Irene swallowed and pushed her chair back. She left her half empty coffee on the counter.

"I gotta run."

The man nodded and started to wipe down the counter with a small towel.

"Don't we all," he said.

✶

Irene made it to the ocean. Night had fallen, and it was cold enough that her clothes felt as though they'd been dipped in a large ice bucket. She stood on the pier and watched the black ocean froth on the shore line. She felt a heaviness, and thought of her family again. Her father and mother, her little brother Terrance. They weren't bad people. And they meant well, but they just didn't understand her. Irene wanted her life to be meaningful. And she just couldn't find meaning in college, where she would spend a hefty amount of her parent's earnings on a degree that permitted her to spend her life in a cubicle or at best, a stuffy office. She admitted that she didn't know how she was to make a living, but wasn't that what part of living was? Figuring things out as you went? She thought so, and as she watched the sea give and take, she felt that the ocean and nature were on her side too. Still, she missed her family. But the last argument they'd had hurt her deeply, and she had to leave. She'd find a job and make her way somehow.

What bothered her most was that tomorrow was Christmas. She'd never spent Christmas away from her family (except for two years ago when she left to her ex-boyfriend's house for a whole week while his mom was away in Israel).

She thought about S.T.E.A.M. She'd never used it, but she really missed her family. Maybe this could be her last chance to see her family before Christmas was over. Sure, it wasn't exactly real. It wouldn't be them in there. But it would feel real to her. And Irene felt that even that would mean a lot to her right now. Because now, standing here surrounded by the sounds of waves and wind and birds, she felt utterly alone.

"Maybe just for Christmas dinner," she thought aloud.

Her family had a tradition of waiting till midnight on Christmas Eve to have their Christmas dinner. It was almost a sacred event in their household, and Irene just felt wrong about passing it up. She missed the old days, when she was younger and her family was closer, and understood each other. Now, with the sneaky way that S.T.E.A.M. had corrupted people's minds, she felt as if her family had changed completely. Her father, for instance, was obviously cheating on her mother. Irene thought it was so obvious. And the worst part was that Dad didn't show any signs of guilt or remorse. And her mother, a whole other case, was very suicidal and would sometimes simulate her own funeral just to see how her loved ones might react in that situation. Irene knew about this because she'd overheard an argument that her parents had had concerning it. She could tell, too, by the way her mother would wander around the house like a ghost. Looking like she didn't belong. Maybe she didn't. Irene herself could attest to not belonging either. Which is why she was here now. But still . . . she missed them. And wanted to continue the Christmas tradition if only to not sink into depression herself.

She walked over to a music store nearby—it was well-lit inside and had different aisles of music and even some movies racked up against the left wall. There were posters of actors and rock bands rolled up and shoved in a large mesh bin, sticking out like baguettes. The store clerk, a thin middle-aged man with glasses and a large brown beard—nodded to her and continued reading his colorful science fiction magazine. There was music playing around the whole store, and Irene could see the speakers, but she didn't recognize the artist. She made her way to the back and found the store's S.T.E.A.M. room. These days, every franchise carried the machine, and even some smaller businesses.

She felt an odd sensation entering the room, and for a moment she was a little uneasy. It felt like she was preparing to take a psychedelic drug and go on a trip. She realized, in a way, that that wasn't too far from the truth.

"Hey, we close in five minutes," the bearded man called from his same spot behind the glass counter.

Irene turned head to see him and nodded in understanding. He waved her on and returned to his pulp magazine.

She lay down on the bed and put the crown on her head. It reminded her of Jesus wearing his crown of thorns. This, however, seemed much less noble.

✳

She was at home. She could hear "Away In A Manger" playing on the radio and already see the firelight flickering over the walls, making light swim around the room like a yellow ocean.

She then smelled her mom's lamb cooking in the oven and the sweet odor of blueberry cheesecake. She turned hastily to see her mom, wearing a yellow apron, standing over the sink, washing her hands.

"Mom," she said.

Her mother looked up, her smooth features looking even more delicate in the soft light of the kitchen. Her brown hair was tied back.

"Baby," she said. "Wash your hands and help me serve the plates."

Irene felt a knot in her throat, and her eyes began to sting with brewing tears.

"What's wrong?" her mother asked, lowering the spoon she held.

"Nothing, nothing," Irene muttered, swabbing her eyes and starting to head into the kitchen. "Where's Dad?"

Mom shrugged and smiled. "Your father's somewhere in this house. Where? I haven't the slightest idea."

They set up dinner: lamb, mashed potatoes, sweet peas, roasted kennels and figs, and for dessert, of course, blueberry cheesecake. Her mother liked to keep her dishes simple and healthy, but she knew just how to prepare them to make them taste spectacular. Irene, on the other hand, had never learned to cook much more than a grilled cheese sandwich.

"Go get your brother," she said, and Irene went after laying the last set of utensils down.

She walked through the halls of her house, feeling her face melt as nostalgia crept in. She loved her family, she really did. Why did she always have to run away from her issues? Her family wasn't perfect, that part was obvious. But whose was?

No, that wasn't the root of the problem. It was S.T.E.A.M. That was the issue. That was the evil. It had changed them. All of them. And now, Irene had fallen into the same trap because she missed her family. And instead of going back to her family like she should have, to solve things the real way, she'd done what everyone had done with this fucking machine—she took the easy way out; getting her "quick fix" and never addressing that root. Letting the connection die. Letting reality die. Just because this was easier, and she could imagine her family to be anything she wanted. Imagine herself to be anyone she wanted. Imagine life itself to be her ideal. But . . . that wasn't life, was it? Was all this more beautiful just because it was perfect? Because, in this alternate reality, her parents didn't argue or cheat or do whatever else they did to hurt each other?

What had life been like before S.T.E.A.M? she wondered. Because she'd lived with it for more of her young adult life, she couldn't remember. She tried to imagine it now; a world where actions were just actions, nothing more, nothing less. Where violence meant violence, and love meant love. Where there was no hiding behind the world you create in your mind, but where you were forced, gloriously, to live amongst others and just try your damned best to be a good person.

Irene suddenly felt embittered by the crown she knew was on her head. She felt it, digging into her scalp and pumping lies into her mind. She let herself feel the darkness of it, the evil, and she suddenly leaned against the wall, feeling disgusted.

"It's all a lie," she thought, feeling herself sink into the rabbit hole that was this damned machine.

"Honey," her mother called out from behind her. "Did you get your brother?"

Irene felt her breathing intensify, and she started to feel nauseas.

Suddenly her father came out of the bedroom with a towel wrapped around his waist and his hair wet.

"Sweetie!" he said smiling. "There you are. I've missed you so—"

Suddenly, Irene was pulled out. She was back in the music store. The quiet atmosphere felt like an odd shift, and she had to close her eyes because the room was spinning and she felt like throwing up. After a moment, she sat up. What had happened? Did the store clerk pull the plug? She looked at her watch. She still had three minutes until the store closed. She got up and walked out of the room into the heart of the music store.

"Hey!" she shouted. "What's the matter with you? It's not even ten yet!"

The man looked up from his magazine and stared at her strangely. "What're you yelling at me for? I've been up here the whole time."

"Well the system shut down." Not that Irene particularly minded. She'd wanted out anyway. But not so suddenly that it made her head spin.

"Did it?" the clerk said. He walked over to the machine, passing Irene by. He crouched down and checked the plug. It was in. He tried rebooting the system but nothing happened.

"Shit," he said. "I just got this thing yesterday. Now I'll have to take it back to the engineers."

Suddenly, a huge stone came crashing through the large window of the store front. The sound shattered and battered and crashed and glass fell in like a waterfall. Irene and the clerk turned sharply, covering their ears until the last of the shards and crystals had fallen. They were too stunned to talk. Irene felt her heart throbbing in her chest and even in her veins.

Then a man in a blue suit jumped into the store.

"Unplug your S.T.E.A.M. and roll it out to my truck, now!" he roared, waving a gun at Irene and the clerk.

The clerk was petrified, holding his hands up in defense. "Our machine is down!"

"Down? Down?!" the man screamed, and ran into the small room where the machine was. "Dammit!" he said. "Shit!"

Then he ran out of the store.

"What the hell was that?" Irene said.

"I don't know," the clerk said. "But I think I have to go."

He walked nervously up to the counter and grabbed his car keys, then walked out of the store, stepping over glass that crunched beneath his feet.

Irene was stunned, but soon she found herself walking out too. But before she reached the end of the store, the television above the counter came to life. It was on a red screen that beeped every second.

Then a voice came on. *"We interrupt to bring you an important message,"* the voice said in a robotic tone, while the beeping persisted. *"S.T.E.A.M. has shut down in thirty states and soon will be shut down completely. Please stay in your homes unless it is unsafe to do so. If your home is unsafe, we advise you to leave there and find a citizen you can trust, or if you are unable to do that, a safe place to stay until you are further notified by your government. Government officials, all police and peace keepers, and all medical staff are officially excused of their duties until this issue is resolved. I repeat, do not go to the police or your hospitals for any issues. They will be unable to help you. Stay tuned for any further instructions. Thank you."*

Irene stood dumbfounded for a few minutes, thinking of what to do next. She felt alone and scared, and she knew it was dangerous to be roaming about aimlessly. She decided she would go back to her family. They might be in danger. She had to be with them just in case.

And it didn't take long. While she stood there thinking and waiting on her decision, it didn't take long for the noise to rise in the darkened streets just outside the store. Screams, alarms, cars roaring by, and, even, gunshots.

Irene felt a deep fear that she'd never experienced before. What was to await her out there? How would America function without their fix? Without S.T.E.A.M?

She grabbed a baseball bat from under the cash register and ran home.

PART TWO: LOVE, AMERICAN STYLE

7

Harry Locklin couldn't believe what he'd heard. He was on the couch with his hands dangling over his thighs. His hair was greasy because he hadn't showered in two days.

"I still think you shouldn't have quit," his wife Carla said from the kitchen.

But he had to quit. He worked at a car shop and he couldn't deal with those fucking people anymore. And maybe they couldn't deal with him either—that was the dangerous part. He was in danger just like everybody else. He had to stay calm. He had to stay here. His house was safe. Was it the sanest environment for him? No. Not with his wife nagging him all day. That had to go.

"Honey, did you hear me?" she called.

Yes, that most certainly had to go.

✳

Harry decided to shower; if only to avoid his wife's fucking voice for a few minutes. I can't kill her though, he thought. I can't, I can't. I want to. God I want to.

But he knew that this wasn't a simulator. This was reality. If he killed her now, she'd only be dead. No unplugging. And yes, he despised her. But he loved her too. He didn't want her dead, not for real. He just wanted her to shut the fuck up.

Cut out her tongue, then, a voice whispered to him.

"No! God dammit!" he shouted in the shower.

After a while, once his pores felt exhausted by the hot steam and his muscles felt weary, he shut off the nozzle and dried himself off with a towel. He braced himself before he entered the bedroom. She might be in there. If she is, he thought, don't react.

But he was so used to living off instinct. So used to slinking away to the garage and bashing her brains in. It gave him a rush. It was a drug that cracked openings in his veins and filled them with hate and rage and God he loved it! *Bash bash bash.* The blood, the look, the dead lump he was left with. He loved it. It made him sick to think of himself that way, but he did love it.

He opened the door. His wife was there. Don't say a word, he begged. Please just don't say a word. Let's just go to bed.

His wife looked at him through her glasses, then she scoffed.

"Jesus, Harry, you're using my towel again."

He froze. His anger, carnal and primitive, quickly turned into something else. A different hunger. One he could satisfy without physically hurting her. The towel dropped.

"Harry," she said, looking confused. "What are you doing?"

He looked down and saw that he was erect. Then he smiled.

If I can't bash her brains *in*, he thought, then I'll fuck her brains *out*.

He strode up to her and as she flinched he grabbed her wrists and said "I'm going to fuck you," and she said "Okay," but she was beginning to cry. Harry ripped her shirt apart and pulled her pajama shorts down. Carla was naked and writhing, but letting him do what he wanted because she knew, somewhere deep he knew that she knew, that he would have killed her otherwise. Soon she was plastered against the soft mattress and he was thrusting into her. And she was crying; her tears and saliva soaking the pillow. Thrusting in and out. In and out. And he didn't care that she hated it. Because, in his opinion, this was his mercy on her. He could have just as easily killed her. Instead—thrust, thrust—almost there. Almost there. And just as he was climaxing, the mattress springs crying out, Carla, his wife, relaxed her body. And Harry's eyes opened up as big as moons. And cold blood washed over her. His blood. And she retracted the knife from his ribs. The same swift motion she'd practiced on her husband dozens of times in S.T.E.A.M. But now the knife was real. It was the knife she kept under her side of the mattress every night, because she didn't trust him.

Sandra watched the fan spin above her head. The shadows spun accordingly, following the blades in perfect harmony. It was so majestic it made her feel sick. Her mother had given up on trying to encourage her. And, after a while, let her be for the rest of the night.

She thought about plugging into S.T.E.A.M. again. Maybe that way, at least, she could be at prom, albeit without really being there.

She thought about Michael. He was probably there, at prom, with Sasha or Crystal or Jennifer. The pretty ones. Of course. And they'd be winning the titles of Prom King and Queen.

Who cares, a voice said in her. *It's just a title*. But she couldn't bring herself to concur with the voice. It did matter; she cared. Because it just wasn't fair.

Her mom rapped at the door again.

"What?" Sandra called out.

"Honey . . . something's happened with S.T.E.A.M."

"What do you mean?" Sandra sat up on her bed.

"The news says the system is on a freeze everywhere."

Sandra rose quickly and rushed over to her machine. Not tonight. Don't do this to me tonight, she thought. Not on my prom. My prom.

But the machine was completely shut down. The electronic display was completely shut off, and when Sandra pressed different buttons and tried to restart it, nothing lit up on the screen. It was completely dead.

"Shit," she said.

She went back to her mother and opened the door. Her mother's eyes looked tired and worn out, with dark bags smiling sadly under each eye.

"What do we do?" Sandra said. "Are they going to send us a new one?"

Her mother shook her head and sniffled with wet mucus in her nostrils. "No honey," she said. "There won't be anymore. Somebody knows how to shut it down. The news said it'll take months before they can develop a system to block out whoever is doing this."

Sandra felt her heart sink. "Then they have to find him," she said.

"They're trying, honey."

"And they have to kill him."

"They're trying, honey."

✳

Sandra sat in bed, feeling the room close in around her like a pack of wolves. Prom had started almost an hour ago. There was still time to go. But what a joke that would be. What a joke all of this was. How was she supposed to go there, wearing a mediocre dress that was probably too tight on her fat, fat frame? And with no date, no less. She didn't even have any friends. No real ones, anyway.

She felt a rage suddenly. She felt a heat in her cheeks. She wanted to kill those bastards. Or she wanted to kill herself. Not because she hated herself. She loved herself, she thought, and thought she deserved better. She hated God, or whoever made her. Because they'd done so unjustly. And now, she hated the person who so carelessly shut down S.T.E.A.M.

But finding him would be an impossible task. If the US government was having trouble doing it, her chances would be a thousand times lower.

But Sandra really couldn't imagine herself being this way for as long as it would take to fix the system. She needed to feel beautiful again. And that, whether she loved or hated herself, was something she knew she wasn't.

If she were hooked up to the machine, she might have gone to kill them. Maybe. Why not? But not now, not when killing them meant they'd actually be dead.

But . . . she couldn't face them on Monday, when school started again. To walk in those halls, everyone laughing about what a great time they had. And to see the looks on their face as she passed them. Looks of pity, looks of empathy, and in some faces, stifled laughter. She just couldn't do it.

She began to cry, watching the walls of her room blur away as tears filled her eyes. In her room, she could already hear the noise in the streets. It sounded like a war. A war she wanted no part in.

Sandra rose from her bed, wiping her tears with trembling hands, and went over to the bathroom. She found the bottle of pills in a long cabinet under the sink. Pills she'd been collecting discreetly from her mother's medicine cabinet for a night like this. They were in an orange bottle and full to the top. She took off the top and stared at the little pills. So small and so deadly. They were white and round and looked chalky. And they could set her free. If there is an afterlife, maybe it's something like S.T.E.A.M. But better, because you can't wake up.

She began to take pill after pill. With heavy tears falling from her eyes. Toss, drink, swallow. Toss, drink, swallow. Toss, drink, swallow. Toss, drink, swallow. Over and over. Until the bottle was empty. She felt panic settle in, but she tried to remind herself that she wanted this. There was nothing left for her here. She knew that it was silly, in a way. It was only a high school prom. But prom represented more to her. It represented inclusion. It represented being accepted and loved. And she was shunned from all of those things. And she would be for the rest of her life—had she not decided to end it.

"I'm going to die very soon," she whispered, watching her hideous face in the bright mirror.

She went back into her bedroom and sat down. She thought about how she might want to spend her last few minutes on Earth. She decided to pick up a collection of poems by Edgar Allan Poe. She read "The Raven" slowly, letting the words sink in. Soon the words began to get blurry and she put the book down.

Soon, now, she thought. She started to regret her decision. But she pushed that thought away. It had to be done. That stupid fucking prom. That stupid fucking tradition. Those stupid students that couldn't show love to anyone different from them. It had to be done.

Suddenly, and it made her drugged heart skip a beat, her mother knocked on the door again.

Oh mom, she thought. *You're such a beautiful person. I wish I didn't have to leave, just for you.*

"What is it?" Sandra called out, starting to cry again.

Her mother was silent for a moment, then she said: "I got a call from Annabel's mother."

"Yeah?"

Her mother sounded like her lips were almost touching the door on the other side.

"She called about prom," she said. "They had to cancel it because of the whole S.T.E.A.M. mess. Some of the kids were killed. That boy you liked . . . Michael?"

Sandra froze. "Yes?"

"His brother killed him an hour ago."

Sandra stared dumbly at the door, feeling her mind split apart. Prom was cancelled. Michael was dead The monster, the fiend, the devil was cancelled. Gone.

Stupid stupid stupid you deserve to die you stupid idiot you deserve it now you.

She felt her muscles tense, and her heart was beating so fast and burning, and her vision was so blurry that she couldn't see the doorknob on the door. Or the knob turning as her mother walked in. When she entered, Sandra was already writhing on the bed, foaming at the mouth. Her mother screamed.

Sandra was dead in seconds, even as her fat body twitched once more.

9

Grandpa Dylan had been in the nursing home for almost a week. His son and that damned wife of his had seen it fit to put him here—no, *force* him here—after they'd discovered that he hadn't exactly overcome his alcohol addiction, but had used S.T.E.A.M. to hide it. And, in doing that so often, had become addicted to the machine as well. He didn't understand their anger, just like they couldn't understand his. He'd done his best, and sometimes in life you had to trade one addiction for another. Life was about coping, and getting by; not about being perfect.

He squeezed the strain on his forehead with his thumb and index finger, closing his eyes and breathing in deeply.

Someone ran by the closed door. Richard Dylan could hear the chirps like a small bird as the (probably nurse's) small feet scurried down the hall.

Richard sat up slowly, feeling his muscles ache. When his elbows were fully extended, he could see the sun beaming from the outside into his room. The room was a bland white place, with minimal brownish-gray furniture and a television set that hung high up and was bolted onto the wall.

"What was *that*?" he said, forcing his old limbs to stand up. He put on his slippers and shuffled up to the door. He opened it.

The hall was completely empty, and almost immediately he could hear some of the elderly people—the bed-ridden ones—calling out from their rooms. He wobbled slowly through the halls, his hands sliding down the white walls to keep his balance. Everyone—all the nurses and staff on that floor—had vanished. What had happened while he was asleep today? And who had gone by running through the hall? He thought maybe it was a nurse.

Then he got another thought. This was his chance to leave here! He could finally escape!

Richard took the elevator down to the first floor, and carefully walked out. He was able to walk better today, because he'd taken some pills that the nurse had left for him on the table last night. Still, he was walking lethargically because he didn't want to be seen. His eyes wandered sharply, scanning the halls he passed—nobody in sight—until he was at the entrance. Where the hell was everyone? he thought again, starting to worry now.

No matter; he was free now!

He shielded his face with a trembling arm as the sun tossed rays of heat over him. He had no car, but he found a golf cart in the parking lot; one of the ones that the security guards of the nursing home would use if anyone unauthorized tried to get in or, in more cases, come out.

The keys were still inside and he switched it on. Richard drove out the parking lot, feeling the wind press cool air at his face, in a pulsating rhythm, making his ears throb.

It was very soon that he noticed the mess in the streets. Even in the beautiful backdrop of blue sky and green trees, the road was littered with people and crashed cars. When he turned the cart onto a major street, he saw some people running and yelling. Some were fighting. One man kicked open a door to a flower boutique and ran in. A second later, Richard heard a gunshot and saw a flash of light behind the glass of the store. On the other side of the street, a man in his—it seemed- fifties, grabbed a teenage girl and tossed her against the hood of a blue parked sedan, then the man pulled down his pants and the girl's skirt and began thrusting into her while the girl screamed and cried.

Richard felt a gushing river of fear come over him. He wanted to help but he was too old. Had S.T.E.A.M. really caused all this? Or rather, the lack of S.T.E.A.M.? Where was the police? The army? Where was the justice? It was only a silly machine. Like a video game.

Abruptly, a body fell right in front of Richard's golf cart. He heard a smack like when he was a child and would smack his open palm against the calm water at the beach. The ground thumped a little. And an arm flew against the hood of the cart. Richard stopped the cart, feeling his weak heart race at a thousand miles an hour. The man who'd jumped the apartment building and killed himself was mostly dressed in blood now, looking more like a grotesque pasta dish than a person. Richard wanted to throw up. He was reminded of the war again. But this seemed worse. At least the war meant something. They'd been fighting for something good. This was just senseless chaos. He stood from the cart and felt like he was going to faint. His vision became narrow and he felt the world closing in on him. Then he turned and saw it.

JAX WINE & SPIRITS, the sign of the store said. Through the glass he could see it all, neatly organized. Bottles going up to the ceiling like ladders to heaven.

No, his logic spoke. *This isn't a simulator anymore. This is real life.* Then another voice countered: *Look around you. You think this is real life? This* is *S.T.E.A.M! This world has always been S.T.E.A.M!*

He heard a gunshot. It was the man who'd raped the teenager. She was dead on the sedan now, blood flowing down the hood and dripping over the cement.

He heard a chuckle in his mind as sanity's cord was clipped and his feet marched to the liquor store.

This is the American dream, baby!

His hands kept exchanging from the pockets of his khakis to the straps of his back pack. Eddie Loffman kept a comfortable distance from Casey as she treaded down the school front steps, making her two-mile trek (which Eddie knew the route of very well). Normally she would just need to walk three blocks, but the buses were out of service now.

S.T.E.A.M. had been down for three full days and it was finally the school's turn to shut down their services. While the government was still relatively in control, there were too many teachers who'd just opted out of their duties, and little by little students just stopped showing up as well. Eddie and Casey were among the few that kept showing up. Casey—Eddie discovered—was only doing it because she needed a place to be away from her abusive father. She hadn't found a good hideout yet and her best friend Chloe said she wouldn't be able to help her until the weekend when she and her family got back from Ontario.

Eddie was only in school to see Casey. And to plan out his scheme. Because now that the country was at war with each other, it was his time to strike. After that first experience with S.T.E.A.M., when he had sex with Casey, he'd done so again about seven times—twice in the teacher's lounge, and a few times at a convenience store near his house that never carded. He needed it again. Needed to fuck her again. At least one more time. This time would be more difficult, because she would surely fight him off, screaming and thrashing and clawing and biting, he could see it in his sizzling mind, but Eddie thought that might actually turn him on more. That was something he was never able to perfect in S.T.E.A.M. The rush of being denied. He thought he might enjoy that more. Possibly. He would find out soon.

He watched her from a block away, and saw her pull out a cigarette and light it as she walked. As she did so, her steps became slower and tighter, and he could see her butt flexing and shifting slowly. He didn't even know that she'd taken up smoking again, but under the circumstances, he figured it didn't warrant too much of a shock.

Eddie was beginning to sweat when he finally saw her turn the key to her house and enter it. He waited and thought of how he would attack. The idea of attacking the girl of his dreams repulsed him, but it was either that or never feel the inside of her sweet, warm pussy again. And that was just something he couldn't live with.

He watched her from the window near the living room. She was walking upstairs, calling her dad's name. There was a feathery tremble in her voice, as if she didn't want her father to answer back.

Then she disappeared from view. Eddie waited, thinking he might have to break the window since the front door was locked. He looked around for a large stone. He found one, but then he heard a scream.

It was Casey.

Eddie quickly picked up the stone and hurled it through the window. He was accidentally too close and felt some glass cut his arm and forehead. He hissed and kicked the remaining glass until there was a big enough opening for him to jump through. He was running upstairs now, watching the stairs hurry beneath him in a blur, and listening as Casey's screams soon became replaced with muffled cries. There were three bedrooms upstairs, all lined in a row with all the doors open. The floor was carpet so he didn't worry too much about having to sneak around. Maybe she'd found her father dead.

But as Eddie entered the room, he found that he was wrong.

Her father was very much alive, and he was holding a knife to Casey's throat.

✱

The disheveled-looking man glared at Eddie confusedly, his feet shuffling back and forth like he was doing some tribal dance. Casey's eyes were giant flares of fear, staring up at Eddie with half-confusion and half-relief that he'd found her.

Eddie raised his arm up slowly. "Let her go," he said.

The man shook his head aggressively and clutched his daughter's waist tighter.

"Get out of here, kid. Who are you? Get out of here!"

Eddie's mind seemed frozen, and he had no idea what his next move should be. He looked to the right and saw a custom made S.T.E.A.M. machine in the form of a queen size bed. There was even a brass-colored headboard and a comforter over it.

Eddie had an idea.

"You don't have to do this," he began, feeling coldness in his hands.

The man grunted and cocked his head to the side, then grunted again. "Get out of here, kid. I'm not going to tell you again."

"I know how to make it work."

The man's eyes lit up, and his fingers loosened slightly on the knife.

"Liar."

"I'm not lying," Eddie said. "I'll prove it. But you have to lie down."

The man grinned, revealing hidden wrinkles under his eyes and cheeks that Eddie hadn't noticed before. His face was sun-burnt and charred, especially around his eyes and forehead. His hair was dark and thin like the short, fine strands of thread that stick out of the buttons of a shirt. His eyes, blood shot and shivering, seemed to only see through the lens of S.T.E.A.M.

And Eddie had to somehow take him there again.

"You expect me to believe you?" Casey's father said.

Casey, meanwhile, was quivering and starting to cry.

"I don't expect anything. I'm just here to tell you what I know. Which is why I came here. To tell Casey."

Her dad flitted his eyes to her, then looked back at Eddie. "You know this kid?"

She nodded tepidly, the knife scraping against her soft neck.

Eddie felt a short-lived pleasure at having Casey say she knew him, but then realized that she was only playing along with his game. A game that was the difference between her living and dying.

"How does it work? The TV said the system was shut down."

Eddie nodded and took a step to the machine, which was also the bed. He decided to bullshit the whole thing. His mind was racing and he didn't know what else to do. So he started making up a lot of nonsense and tried throwing in words to confuse the man. Hoping he'd be stupid and desperate enough to believe him.

"The system that connects the processors to the server might not work, sure, but the generator doesn't run by that alone. S.T.E.A.M. works with the mind, and that's something the government can never shut down . . ." Bullshit and gibberish, but the man's eyes seemed to be eating it up, and he looked hopeful. He was desperate for any answer.

"You see," Eddie went on, watching the man's knife lower. "The brain has electrical charges that stimulate the crown in S.T.E.A.M. If you can get enough of those charges flowing, you won't need the server or the system. All you need is what's already in your head."

The man was already moving Casey aside and staring at his bed with hungry eyes. He wanted to go back. Just as everyone in America wanted to go back. And he was willing to let himself believe the lie if it meant having a chance.

"Okay," he said. "Guide me. Plug me in. Take me there."

Eddie smiled and nodded, rubbing the heavy stone that he still carried behind his back.

"We'll go there together," he said.

✳

Her father lay down, and his hands looked utterly re-laxed for the first time since Eddie had met the man. He closed his eyes and Eddie placed the crown on his head.

"Now this is going to work like hypnosis. It won't be an easy process. But I promise you'll be back there soon and it'll be worth it."

The man was smiling like someone waiting to open their eyes to a surprise party. In many ways his expectations were similar to just that.

"Now breathe in," Eddie suggested, while Casey watched nervously behind him.

"Slowly and effortlessly. Let your mind become blank."

The man looked so relaxed that his eyes took on the stillness of an inanimate object. Perhaps a lamp or a sea shell.

Eddie, on his end, began to raise the stone in his left hand. Casey saw this and yelped, but then kept her mouth shut.

"What do you see?" Eddie asked, his hand above him.

"I see . . . yes!" cried the man. "I see a room. And a mirror. And the crown on my head. The silver crown!"

"Good . . ." Eddie whispered."Now let your body sink into that place."

"Yes," he said softly. "Okay. I can do that."

The man began to smile more broadly. Then, Eddie lowered the stone fiercely. It crashed on the man's skull.

Casey cried out.

"He's not dead," Eddie said, checking the pulse. "I wasn't trying to kill him. Just knock him out."

Casey was panting and crying in the corner of the room, near the door and a poster of one of her favorite indie bands.

Eddie went up to her and placed his hands on her shoulders. They were quaking and throbbing insanely.

"Shhhhh . . ." he said. "You'll be okay. I'm going to take care of you now."

Casey tried to stifle her tears, and did finally, then smiled up at him. She felt safe at last, he knew. He made her feel safe.

"I'm going to take care of you," he said again.

But the way he was looking at her. Her smile faded. She fell back against the glossy papery poster.

He locked the door before she could reach it.

Casey screamed from inside the room.

Ryan and Amy stumbled down the dark streets of New Jersey. They made it to a small park with a rusty playground sitting on a wooden perimeter filled with sand. The sand was cold as it seeped into Amy's sandals. Ryan sat on the swing. It whistled as he rocked back and forth. Amy sat on the other swing. It didn't whistle because she sat still.

"We're poor again," she said. "Now we'll always be poor."

Ryan looked up and saw the purple trees painted in moon-dusted shadows.

"We don't need all that to be happy."

"Don't be a fool," she said. "Money doesn't buy happiness? That's a lie to keep poor people content. Money buys everything."

"We can loot," Ryan said. "There's no police now. No nothing. We can loot if we want."

"Of course we'll loot. That's not the point. Everyone is going to loot. You know what that means? We'll still be at the bottom. We'll always be at the bottom."

"But we'll still have things if we loot."

"You idiot," she said.

They sat, and Ryan stopped rocking. He dug his shoes into the sand.

"Why do we need things to be happy?"

"Because life doesn't run without things. Why does a car need oil to run? Why do you need eyes to see? We need things to be happy. Because life isn't so great without those things."

"That's stupid," Ryan said. "That doesn't make any sense. Tell that to monks who are happy eating donated peas and soup once a week."

"Well they're fools too. You need things to be happy."

"You don't know what you're talking about."

"Are you happy?" she said, gripping the chain of the swing with her left arm.

"You know the answer."

"So you're not."

"Of course I'm not."

There were screams in the avenues nearby.

"Then shut up," she said. "Let's go before they take all the good stuff."

✳

The streets were filled. Ryan couldn't understand how things had gotten so bad so fast. Gunshots were heard popping in the dark sky. People were shoving each other and punches were thrown, glass lay scattered on the streets like Mardi Gras beads. Everyone held either a weapon or something they'd stolen. And in some cases when their strength permitted it, both.

Ryan couldn't understand how S.T.E.A.M., essentially a form of entertainment, could cause such havoc in the entire country. It almost didn't make sense. How did people live without it before? How did Ryan live without it? And he had. At least for the first fifteen years of his life. But now, he couldn't remember a time when he had to suppress any desire of his—good or bad. This is how the country had been raised. They took what they wanted. And now, stripped of S.T.E.A.M., the evidence was right before his eyes.

"There's nothing in there!" Amy cried, rushing out of an electronic goods store.

"What'ju expect?" Ryan shot back, feeling small in the littered streets.

"Come on!"

"Where are we going?"

"We need stuff! We need something!"

"Why?" he asked.

"Come on!"

✳

They searched for hours. Eventually, they pulled a van they'd stolen from an Asian woman into an alley and sat still in the car.

"We got some value back there," Amy said.

"Great."

"Now what?"

"What do you mean?"

"What do we do with it now?"

"What do you mean?" he asked, looking back at the five large sacks of things. "We use it."

"That's it?" She sounded disappointed.

"What else do you do with stuff?"

"I don't know."

"No, you don't. Are you happy now?"

"No."

"No. So what would help?"

"Maybe a house," she said. "Or a car."

"Or an island of your own? I can't stand you."

She put the car in reverse and backed out of the alley.

"I think just a bigger house will make me happy," she said. "Somewhere we can put this shit."

12

Irene ran. Her thigh muscles felt like hot air balloons, but like the heat would soon cause the balloons to burst. Her arms raced rapidly at her sides, and she felt the sweat that was forming in her pores sprint off her skin and fall behind her. The cool morning air was pressing on her face and ears, making a sound in her head like driving with the windows lowered.

But she was not alone on these streets. Far from it. Often she had to dodge other people who were either running or driving maniacally. She saw one car three blocks ahead just plow into a herd of people; people who shouted and cried as their bodies were hurled in the air. She felt her heart bolt inside her chest, threatening to explode inside her.

Then came the tears.

She couldn't contain them, especially when thinking about her family. Now more than ever she realized how much she really needed them. How much she needed them to be okay. To be safe. And now . . . nobody was safe.

She tried to slap her face gently to swipe away the tears, which were skewing her vision. There was a gas station to her right and she saw a motorcycle crash into a car parked there. It was going so fast that Irene knew it had to be some attempt at suicide. The man on the bike was flung like a rock from a slingshot and splattered against the wall near the restroom door. His body actually stayed stuck on the wall for a couple of seconds before it fell onto the ground—first his arms fell off the wall, then his head, then his torso, all in separate pieces. There was a tapestry of blood and guts on the wall.

She turned her head away, feeling dizzy, and fought the urge to vomit. She had to get home.

"Mom," she mumbled behind her breath, her body bouncing. "Dad. I'm coming."

✳

The sun was high in the sky now. She'd stolen a bike from a toy store and rode it for about eight miles, then stopped at another gas station. She dropped the bike once she was under the pavilion. This part of town seemed empty, and Irene was relieved. She pushed the door of the convenience store open and heard a little chime go off, announcing her entrance.

Nobody was inside. Good.

She went to the fridge and grabbed a bottle of red Gatorade. She downed it in an instant. Then she grabbed another and drank that one, but slower. Then she grabbed a large water bottle to put on her bike for later.

As she was perusing the snacks aisle, and nibbling on a beef jerky, the television set in the store came to life. There was a resonant beeping sound and a blue screen with white letters. Irene stared at the words, dumbfounded. Her hands felt icy and her stomach was in knots.

THE UNITED NATIONS HAVE QUARANTINED AND DECLARED NUCLEAR WAR ON THE UNITED STATES OF AMERICA.

That's all that the screen said. No instructions. No details, like when, or why.

Well, Irene knew why. Even if S.T.E.A.M. could've been fixed in two weeks or so, the country couldn't last that long. This was America's drug. They did what they wanted, when they wanted. And now that they were cut loose, let out of their cages, America was a liability to the rest of the world.

Irene still couldn't move, feeling as if the soles of her feet were rooted to the ground.

Then she thought of her family again, and that this might be the last day she ever got to see them again, and uprooted her feet and ran like hell.

✳

She reached her house faster than she'd expected to. Her mind was far off as she ran. She thought of the whole country being obliterated, and the rest of the world going on after as if America was all just a bad dream.

The American dream. Or to the rest of the world, the American nightmare. Who was to blame? The people? The government which made S.T.E.A.M. legal? No . . . probably not. They'd had good intentions. They wanted to lower crime by allowing people to do evil elsewhere. It was a good plan, Irene thought. But it had definitely backfired.

She entered her house carefully, twisting the knob of the front door and hearing the familiar whine of the old hinges. Everything looked normal. Nothing seemed broken or messy at all.

As she walked over to the kitchen, she saw a large note taped on the wall. It was recorded on an electronic note, which flashed until she clicked the receiving button. Suddenly the words illuminated on the page.

Dear Irene,

We hope this letter finds you well. Not everything is well here, I'm afraid. Your mother has passed away. I'm crying badly because I think it was my fault. We had gotten into an argument at Christmas dinner and she started to choke on something. I didn't know how to help, and neither did your brother, but we tried. But I blame myself because it was a stupid argument and I started it.

Anyway, your brother and I are driving down to North Carolina to bury her. She wanted to be buried with her parents, if you remember.

I'm sorry for all of this. You were right to run away. But we miss you terribly. I don't know why we needed S.T.E.A.M. at all. We did well once without it. But when something like that is introduced, one gets a taste and suddenly can't live without it. Americans are such an evil breed, my baby. Maybe if people were honest about that things would've ended differently.

Well, we have to leave before it gets dark. We're taking the truck. If we see you along the path we will stop to get you. If you're reading this now and want to meet us in Wilmington Beach, please do so. You remember Grandpa's house, right? Of course you do. Watching the beach from the parlor window was your favorite place in the world. You didn't need S.T.E.A.M. for that.

We love you, sweetie.
-Dad

Irene lowered the electronic note. She felt stiff. *Choked.* In all this havoc, her mother died in such a meager way.

She walked around the living room table and saw that it was messy with empty, dirty plates and cups.

They were probably in too much of a rush after dinner to even bother cleaning up. No matter, they wouldn't see this place again. Irene predicted that this war was probably going to commence soon. And no doubt America would lose against the rest of the world. Would her country even fight back? Probably not. All the important people were probably already halfway across the world by now, getting front row seats to the light show.

No, the American citizens were alone now. Abandoned, as they'd always been.

Irene went into the patio, which is where they kept their S.T.E.A.M. machine. She closed the patio door gently and watched the orange sky as the sun hung limp behind the battered clouds. Soon now, she thought. Very soon.

She tried to empty her mind, because she didn't want to think about it anymore. All the people that would die when this bomb struck. America left behind in dust while the rest of the world went on to future endeavors.

She opened the S.T.E.A.M. bed lid, and lay inside. Her head was heavy on the pillow, and she placed the crown on.

She breathed deeply and slowly, letting herself relax. She waited for a couple of minutes, thinking about her dead mother. They were probably near Virginia by now. They probably wouldn't make it to the grave on time. That was a shame.

And it was true, because suddenly Irene heard a thunderous sound that made her shudder. Her head turned slight to the right. Past the patio pavilion, and the yard, somewhere deep far on the horizon, she saw a mushroom cloud burst up from the ground like a sea monster emerging from the ocean. There it was. Her glazed eyes watched it closely, and the cloud had the face of Death.

Irene turned her head back and closed her eyes, letting S.T.E.A.M. take her someplace else. Because although S.T.E.A.M. was gone, it had always been alive in her mind.

In a flash of heat, the bomb swept over her, and America dreamed.

SERVA ANIMUM CASTELLUM CUSTODITUM · HORTUM BENE CURATUM · FLUMEN NON OBSTRUCTUM ·

Did you enjoy the book?

We welcome all feedback and queries.
Villipede.com

Benjamin Card is a 26-year-old horror and sci fi writer from Miami, Florida. From a young age he's been writing comic books and unfinished stories, but most of his recent inspiration has come from 50s and 60s writers such as Richard Matheson, Rod Serling, and Ray Bradbury, along with other horror writers such as Shirley Jackson, Stephen King, and Sam Raimi. *The Twilight Zone* and *The Evil Dead* were probably his most defining inspirations, and he hopes to one day gain a similar level of respect for his own works.

When he's not creating screwed up worlds in his mind, Benjamin can be found writing music for his rock band, My Flesh Heart, or for the new church he and his uncle created, Included Church. He also works part-time at two different funeral homes (of course he does).

PS: Don't forget to leave a review on Amazon, BN.com, or Goodreads!